A Stash

CW00419366

Edited by

With contributions ~~by~~ ~~the entrants in the 2015~~
Worcestershire Literary Festival
Flash Fiction Competition

Thanks and acknowledgements to Judges:
Calum Kerr http://www.calumkerr.co.uk
Lindsay Stanberry-Flynn
http://lindsaystanberryflynn.co.uk

This anthology is brought to you by
The Worcestershire Literary Festival
Flash Fiction Team www.worcslitfest.co.uk

Black Pear Press

A Stash of Flashes
Worcestershire Literary Festival
Flash Fiction Competition Anthology 2015

First published in November 2015 by Black Pear Press
www.blackpear.net

Compiled & edited by:
Black Pear Press

ISBN 978-1-910322-20-8

Cover Design by Black Pear Press

More Black Pear Press Anthologies

Short Stories:

Seaglass And Other Stories

A collection of short stories from various authors who entered the first Black Pear Press short story competition 2014.

Paperback ISBN: 978-1-910322-14-7
eBook ISBN: 978-1-910322-15-4

Short Stories From Black Pear - Volume 1

A collection of short stories from various Worcestershire-based authors including humour, true life, science fiction, horror and some almost impossible to categorise.

Paperback ISBN: 978-0-9927755-0-6
eBook ISBN: 978-0-9927755-2-0

Flash Fiction:

Fifty Flashes 2014

Winners and selected entries from the Worcestershire LitFest & Fringe Flash Fiction Competition 2014.

Paperback ISBN: 978-1-910322-10-9
eBook ISBN: 978-1-910322-11-6

Flashes of Fiction 2013

Winners and selected entries from the Worcestershire LitFest & Fringe Flash Fiction Competition 2013. Write a short story in under 300 words—73 different stories in one book.

Paperback ISBN: 978-0-9927755-1-3
eBook ISBN: 978-0-9927755-3-7

Fifty Flashes of Fiction
Winners and selected entries from the Worcestershire
LitFest & Fringe Flash Fiction Competition 2014.
Paperback ISBN: 978-1-910322-10-9
eBook ISBN: 978-1-910322-11-6

Young Writers - Aged 7 - 17

Worcestershire Young Writers Competition Anthology 2014
Read the early work of budding fiction writers:
Winners and selected entries from the Worcestershire
Young Writers Competition 2014.
Paperback ISBN: 978-1-910322-12-3
eBook ISBN: 978-1-910322-13-0

www.blackpear.net

Competition Winners

The Worcestershire Literary Festival Flash Fiction Competition 2015 and The Flash Fiction Team announced the ten shortlisted finalists in the competition at the Festival launch event in June 2015 (alphabetical order):

Wendy Bastable	*Crying Over You*
Tracy Fells	*Snake*
Bronwen Griffiths	*Diving Board*
John Holland	*Sensitive*
Susan Howe	*Separation*
Jane Anne Rogers	*The Work Of A Heartbeat*
Diane Simmons	*From Memory*
Diane E Tatlock	*Hidden Views*
Diane E Tatlock	*The Kingfisher*
Suz Winspear	*Teatime With Zombies*

These stories are the first ten in this anthology followed by those who were longlisted or selected by the founder and a judge of this competition, Lindsay Stanberry-Flynn.

Judges, Calum and Lindsay awarded:

First prize to John Holland *Sensitive*
Second prize to Diane E Tatlock *The Kingfisher*
Third prize to Bronwen Griffiths *Diving Board*

Introduction

Welcome to the fourth Worcestershire LitFest and Fringe flash fiction anthology. It is hard to believe that 2015 marked the festival's fourth flash fiction competition. What started as a glimmer of an idea back in December 2011 is now an established and highly successful part of the writing competition calendar. Equally, the anthology produced annually is eagerly awaited, and this year is no exception. The anthology contains a selection of flash fictions that were submitted to the competition, and is published once again by Black Pear Press, Worcestershire's very own small publisher.

The number of entries for 2015 held steady, and as in previous years they came not only from all over the UK, but also from more far-flung countries. Calum Kerr, founder of National Flash Fiction Day, and I had the enjoyable—if at times, difficult—task of judging the entries. As in previous years, we read all the entries and each selected our top fifteen. From those, a shortlist of ten was drawn up and the three winners selected. Thanks to Calum for his expertise and hard work.

Obviously we were looking for stories that were well-written, but flash fiction is a difficult craft to master. For me, the ideal flash has to take me into its own world. I want to learn about the characters, understand something of their lives, and feel their emotions. To achieve all this in three hundred words or fewer is a tall order. Every word has to count, and what's not said is as important as what is. I was looking for a strong voice and a sense of narrative. Even the shortest of stories must be about something.

Our three winners were all successful at meeting the above criteria. Congratulations to our winner, John Holland with his flash 'Sensitive', a thought-provoking and ironic take on the difficulties of personal relationships. Our second prize-winner was Diane E Tatlock with 'The Kingfisher', a flash where the sub-text is suffused with emotion. And our third prize went to Bronwen Griffiths with 'Diving Board', a beautifully-written piece that gets better with each read.

To those and to everyone else who entered their flashes for the competition, I'd like to say thank you. As a writer myself, I know it's not easy to let your work out into the big, wide world, and to have it judged. It is a privilege to be entrusted with your 'babies'.

Last, but by no means least, thank you to the competition co-ordinator, Polly Robinson, who works tirelessly to ensure its continuing success.

Competition Founder and Judge of Worcestershire LitFest Flash Fiction competition
www.lindsaystanberryflynn.co.uk

Contents

More Black Pear Press Anthologies 1
Competition Winners 3
Introduction 4
Contents 7
Sensitive – John Holland 9
The Kingfisher – Diane E Tatlock 10
Diving Board – Bronwen Griffiths 11
Crying Over You – Wendy Bastable 12
Snake – Tracy Fells 13
Separation – Susan Howe 14
The Work Of A Heartbeat – Jane Anne Rogers 15
From Memory – Diane Simmons 16
Hidden Views – Diane E Tatlock 17
Teatime with Zombies – Suz Winspear 18
Broken – Walburga Appleseed 19
The Mission – Wendy Bastable 20
Where Dreams Became Nightmares – Anne Bathurst 21
Knowing – Jan Baynham 21
A Villainous Happily Ever After – Gemma Jean Bennett 22
Black and White? – Kevin Brooke 23
Lost But No One's Looking – John Damien 24
Getting Over Peter – Bren Gosling 25
Could've – Joe Govan 26
Sad Friday – Bronwen Griffiths 27
Sensible Slippers – Anne Harding 27
A Hot Summer's Day – John Holland 28
Fallout – Susan Howe 29
Music To My Ears – Louise Jones 30
Andrew – Tony Judge 31
Left Behind – Lynne Nugent 32
Andrew The Servant – Dunstan Power 32
If Only I'd Married Monty Don – Emma Shaw 34
Art Appreciation – Diane Simmons 35
Her First Steps – Jamie D Stacey 36
The Cull – Tim Stavert 37
Mistaken Identity – Karen Storey 38
Faculty – Richard Westwood 38

The Performance Of Our Lives – Suz Winspear 39
Of Course – Walburga Appleseed 40
Deliverance – Anne Bathurst 41
Standing Up To Barker – Jan Baynham 41
Thinking Outside The Box – Bren Gosling 43
The Million Robot March – Joe Govan 44
The Banker – John Holland 45
Lost – Susan Howe 45
Cop Killer – Tony Judge 46
Dog – Dunstan Power 47
Letter From The Front – Emma Shaw 48
A New Route – Diane Simmons 49
The Love I Don't Tell – Jamie D Stacey 50
Trial Run – Tim Stavert 51
Strawberry Jam – Karen Storey 52
Fraternal Love – Dunstan Power 53
Authors' Biographies 55

Sensitive – John Holland

I'm hyper-sensitive, she said. The psychiatrist told me. Figures, he said. She flew into a rage.

They were going out. You look beautiful, he said. Last week you said I looked very beautiful, she said. They didn't go out.

She wrote. He read it. This is brilliant, he said, but have you thought about…? She'd left the room before he'd finished.

She cooked for him. He added salt to his meal. She didn't speak to him for two days.

He had a night out with his mates. Did you have a nice time, she said. Without me?

He tried.

You look more beautiful than I have ever seen you, he said. They went out. He knew he'd never top that.

I love you, he said. You have told me twice today, but three times yesterday, she said. Today isn't over yet, he said.

You're writing is brilliant, he said. She smiled.

This meal is wonderful, he said. She laughed.

Honesty and openness were ground into the eggshell floor.

I'm bored, she said. Let's break up.

But I love you, he said (for the third time that day).

The next day she asked him why he'd stopped crying.

Years later, they bumped into each other.

How are you? she asked.

Very well, he said.

Angry, she walked away.

The Kingfisher – Diane E Tatlock

Sophie threw down her scooter, ran inside. Decision made.

'Coming for a walk, Auntie Dee?'

'OK, Sophie. Not far though, my leg's still a bit sore from that fall I had.'

'What about down the woods by the river? Mum's favourite. A kingfisher lives there.'

'Lovely.' Dee stopped sorting through her sister's things, offered Sophie a pendant. 'Here, take this. It was your mum's—her birthstone. Put it on.'

Sophie took Dee's hand, leading the way.

'Wish Mum was here with us,' she said, stepping carefully. 'Mum thought you could make her better, didn't she?'

'I did try. Used positive thinking, touched her where her body was betraying her.'

'She still left us though,' Sophie sniffed. 'Dad says the doctor's way would have worked, could have saved her.' She hung back, kicked the dead leaves.

'Your mum was happy for the time she was given.' Dee reached for Sophie's hand again. 'Come on now, let's find that kingfisher.'

The woods were dark.

'Which way now, Sophie?'

'Down by the river. Nearly there now.'

Water swirled over the boulders. Rushing. Deep.

'This is it. The kingfisher's often here. Mum and I saw it loads of times.'

'Oh, you're so lucky. I'd really love to see it.'

'Come over here then. Stand on that stone.'

Dee stepped forward. A flash of turquoise darted from the bushes. Brilliant plumage skimmed among the spray.

The panic-stricken scream followed its path.

Sophie stood. Watching. Gazing along the river, over the waterfall. She raised her hand and waved.

'Mum always told me to mind that slippy stone. You really should have known that, Auntie Dee.' She turned, walked away, spoke over her shoulder. 'Even the kingfisher never sits there.'

Sophie held the jewel Dee had given her up to the sky. The sapphire blazed.

Diving Board – Bronwen Griffiths

Loretta raises her arms in the air, leans forward. Her body hurtles through the echoing space of the swimming pool, a thin, white bird. She hits the water with a splash, goes under, comes up grinning, thumb in the air, kicks her legs, is out and off again.

The boys behind me, shove and grunt. Their familiar accents rise and fall. My toes curl against the edge of the board. I feel the slippery wetness under the soles of my feet, the air chilling my arms. The board springs a little, uncertain.

The water is blue like the postcard that sits on our mantelpiece. But how far away it is.

My teeth chatter. I feel the weight of the boys behind me.

'Gerra move on, won't yow?'

'Urry up. Way ent waiting all day.'

I close my eyes, open them again. Raise my arms like Loretta. She's already at the foot of the diving board, impatient, waiting. I know she's there.

'Curm on!'

My heart is pitter-pattering like raindrops on the roof. I bend my knees, grit my teeth. The board springs up like a trap.

I hit the water sooner than expected. Chlorinated water in my mouth, nose aching. Down here it's another world, a light and heavy world, the sounds of kids coming from miles away, as if they were inside the pipes we like to play in on the way to Hill Pool.

I surface, gasping, choking, eyes stinging. Everything blurry, loud. Loretta is already at the top of the board again, fearless. She'll fly into that water time and time. Every holiday till we're fifteen and she is pregnant but still fearless. Every holiday till we're fifteen and she has bruises and a black eye and is still fearless.

Crying Over You – Wendy Bastable

We'd met, as arranged, for a mid-morning coffee. Fran looked as she always did in my eyes—perfect.

'Remember those espressos in the Park Café when we were teenagers?' I said over our cappuccinos. 'All that steam and foam and the gushing sound of the Italian coffee machine?'

'And the Formica table tops, the red plastic and chrome chairs. And the boys. You, me and the boys,' she enthused.

'You and the boys,' I said.

'Remember those songs? "In dreams." Roy Orbison. We wore the jukebox out playing it.'

"Only in dreams" I certainly remember that…Fran,' I began gently, 'I've been hearing stories about Tom.'

'The big O. His voice was so powerful. "Only the lonely." Do you remember that one?'

'How could I forget it?…Fran, Tom and Eleanor. I think it's been going on for some time.'

She was gazing out of the window and fiddling with the tassels on her scarf.

'And what was his other big hit? Oh yes, "It's over". That was so…' Her voice tailed off. Her eyes had misted over.

'Plaintive?' I hazarded. But I don't think she heard.

'I'm always here, Fran. Always here for you,' I said, holding back that familiar choked up feeling.

Snake – Tracy Fells

Fifty years old, and with funeral politics concluded, I'm tackling the contents of my father's terraced house. Sorting through the rubbish he meticulously hoarded, a memory of my mother is resurrected by the scent escaping as I tug out the bottom drawer of an old chest.

Lily of the Valley.

My mother standing half in shadow at the open door, a smile already fading as she turned away. Immaculate nails, shining like wet rubies, gripped the cream clutch purse that perfectly matched her flared-cut coat and pale cheeks. Coiled around her neck, like an emerald silk snake, was my favourite scarf. The one I always chose for her from the chest of drawers that creaked and complained like a grumbling giant in the corner of my parents' bedroom. Scent lingered from her warm wrists as I played in the yard. Teasing a twist of yarn through the long wet grass for Milly's kittens to pounce upon with needle claws.

After my mother left, an army of female relations took over so a silly little girl didn't bother Father. I only saw her again in the photographs my aunties picked over each Christmas; her image held captive like a creature preserved in amber. Her name never spoken above a whisper.

Now I'm clearing the family home where my father drowned Milly and her five kittens in the basement. Slipping back into childhood I see her again. My mother's silent, red lips closing as she pulled away from his grip. Father's knuckles turning white as his fingers tightened around her wrist. Hissing and cursing, bloated with venom, his ugly words spattered her face.

I lift out the silk scarf. Drape it over my arm. It shimmers like the empty, lifeless skin of some exotic green snake.

Separation – Susan Howe

Lately he has a way of saying goodbye that makes me wonder if I'm losing him. He tries to hide the confusion in his eyes but whether it is over some present or future betrayal is impossible to read. His fingers brush mine and sorrow ripples through my body, ending in a jolt to my heart. He's begun the process of leaving me and there's nothing I can do.

I can't help remembering those blissful days when I was all he needed. When he gazed at me as though I was the only woman he could ever love. It seems only yesterday.

His face is bright with expectation: the burning of something new. I disguise my pain behind a smile and I can tell he appreciates my efforts. He knows I'll make it easy for him. It was the bargain we struck when he came into my life, a sublime but transient gift. I simply never imagined the change would come so soon or hurt so much.

We have almost reached our destination and once again I'm struggling to keep the panic from my voice. I concentrate on breathing, as I was taught. He squeezes my hand, offering comfort despite his growing excitement.

The young woman stands in the entrance wearing a pretty frock and a welcoming smile.

'Hello, Barney,' she says, resting her hand on his shoulder.

His teacher and I share a moment of understanding as I ruffle his hair.

'Have a lovely day, poppet,' I say, wondering whether a kiss would seem too needy.

He glances up as I step back—and there's that look again. Our eyes lock, we connect, and elation mingles with relief as I realise it will take more than another woman to break our bond. I decide to chance that kiss.

The Work Of A Heartbeat – Jane Anne Rogers

The ward was bright with morning sun.

'Could you take the nametag off for me? It feels too tight on him.'

I held the tiny card. Blue for a boy. George James Mulholland. 11/05/1941.

The baby wriggled his fat wrist in protest. Sister Edler was nowhere to be seen.

'Shh,' I whispered.

'It's a little awkward,' I said to his mother.

My own son was asleep.

One kiss.

One hurried blessing.

Two un-knotted tags.

And Thomas became George.

'He's nodded off,' I said, putting him carefully on her lap.

She ran her hand across his chubby arm, her touch light, soft. She smiled and I let myself breathe.

'Waiting for your husband?' I asked.

She nodded. 'You?'

'No. Missing in action.'

I bent and said to baby George/Thomas, 'Your daddy's a hero isn't he?'

She hugged my son close, protecting him from the world.

I bit my lip, remembering the doctor's words. 'Unlikely to reach five…it's in God's hands, Mrs Petheridge.'

Standing, I said, 'I must go. My sister said she'd meet me downstairs.'

And that was it.

A healthy baby.

The child in her arms slept on, exhausted and sickly.

In the corridor I steadied myself against the wall, triumphant, dizzy.

A white coat whirled out.

'Ah! Mrs Mulholland,' he said.

'I wanted to catch you before you went.' He consulted his clipboard.

Breath in, ready to explain. But he spoke first.

'I'm afraid it isn't good news…the ophthalmologist's report suggests…' he said.

Sister Edler appeared. 'No, Dr Matthews…this is the other lady…you know…'

She raised her eyebrows nodding her head towards the tiny boy in my arms.

He shook his head sadly, his hand on my arm. 'I should have remembered. Unforgiveable of me.'

They spun away.

The word floated in the air between us.

'Unforgiveable.'

From Memory – Diane Simmons

Penny is painting lilies when Joanne arrives. Penny smiles at her friend, tries not to show that she minds the interruption. Joanne hugs her. 'You're painting again!'

'People keep bringing me flowers.' She stares at the folded striped shirt Joanne is holding. 'You've brought it back.'

'I'm sorry, but I couldn't even get him to try it on.'

Penny checks her hands are clean and strokes the cotton. 'No one will have it. It's not like Alastair ever wore it. And it came from Harrods.'

When Joanne leaves, Penny unfolds the shirt. The cotton is heavy and her arthritic fingers ache as she smoothes out the creases. It feels luxurious, an extravagant present bought when she still had hope that Alastair would recover.

She holds it up, tries to imagine him wearing it.

The manipulation of the wire mesh takes Penny a month. When the basic shape of the armature is finished, she leaves it for weeks, exhausted by the pain in her hands, unsure after years of not sculpting, whether she still has the strength needed.

When she eventually returns to her studio she is struck by how successful the sculpture is. Even in its early stages, it is Alastair—his slouched sitting position, his drooped head as he reads a book, the way his free hand dangles over the arm of the chair.

She works, covering the mesh in rags, shaping from memory.

When she eases the shirt on to his body it fits perfectly.

Hidden Views – Diane E Tatlock

He watches. From behind trees.

The child plays, oblivious. She clambers on climbing frames, swoops on swings. Runs from the roundabout when her mother calls. Together, they walk away. Holding hands. Laughing. The wife, no longer wife; the daughter, no longer knowing father.

Alone. Behind trees. He no longer watches.

He cries.

Teatime with Zombies – Suz Winspear

The zombie apocalypse was nothing like we'd expected. The films had got it wrong. Yes, zombies do have an insatiable hunger for human brains, but they're easy to outrun, so you'd be unlucky to get bitten. The problem we had was that when they first rose from their graves, the poor things were utterly bewildered. They didn't think about brains right away; they thought they were still human, just really drunk and ravenously hungry, so they did exactly what they would have done in life.

It chanced that the main entrance to our local cemetery was near a fast-food shop selling fried chicken. We now know that any organic matter a zombie bites will become contaminated and will quickly become both zombified and hungry. So when the zombies came swarming out of the cemetery, they all headed straight for the fried chicken shop. The staff and the customers saw them coming and ran away, whilst the zombies broke into the kitchen and raided the fridge.

Zombie chickens are harder to deal with than you might expect. They're surprisingly agile, they peck at anything that moves, and their beaks are sharp enough to draw blood. Several of our clean-up squad got infected that way. Then one chicken somehow got into a broiler house. The sight of twenty thousand zombie chickens pouring out of the shed when the doors were opened, that ravenous look burning in their little red evil eyes, is hard to forget.

Still, we've had it easy here compared to some places. There's a market town in Hampshire where the churchyard was next door to the tearooms, and when the zombies came, Afternoon Tea was just being served.

Zombie Cupcakes…half their clean-up squad are still in therapy.

Broken – Walburga Appleseed

It's been six months. People are talking,' William said. The wind chopped off his words and tugged on Nora's scarf.

'Let them talk.'

Nora kept her hand on the pushchair and her eyes on baby Charlie. His eyelashes cast a shadow on his porcelain cheeks. His fists were just visible at the rim of the blanket. Nora tucked them under.

'You have become obsessed with this baby,' said William. 'We haven't made love for months. How do you imagine we're ever going to be a proper family?'

Mrs Bentley shuffled past. Her dog snuffled up Nora's legs. Mrs Bentley snuffled into the pushchair.

'Such a beauty. Always so quiet,' Mrs Bentley said in her rasping voice.

Nora pulled her lips into an airy smile. William looked the other way. Mrs Bentley shuffled on.

'Come on, Spot,' she said.

William's eyes bore into Nora's.

'What a beauty. Always so quiet,' he rasped.

Nora bent over the pushchair and pulled Charlie against her chest, wrapping the blanket tight around him.

'Nora. Give me the child,' William said.

Nora stepped away, but William caught her by the shoulder and tore Charlie out of her arms.

Nora flushed scarlet.

'Careful you'll hurt him,' she whispered.

'Hell I'll hurt him!'

Mrs Bentley stopped and turned. Spot whimpered.

William raised Charlie high up over his head.

'William, please!' Nora screamed.

William hurled him to the floor.

Baby Charlie cracked and broke into a thousand tiny pieces of porcelain.

Nora plunged, hands outstretched. But her fingers connected only with dust which the wind brushed away almost at once.

The Mission – Wendy Bastable

'You're not from these parts,' she said. 'South Londoner, like me. So what are you doing up here?'

'Oh, you know, escaping from the big city. I needed some space with no responsibilities. So, I'm enjoying the open road for a while.'

It sounded corny. She didn't answer. The gate between us rattled to and fro on its rusty hinges.

'Just working my way through,' I ventured. 'You've a big place here…looks like a lot of work.'

'Yes,' she agreed.

'I could give you a hand for a day or two. Mend some fences, give the woodwork a lick of paint. I can turn my hand to most things. I won't need paying. Just some food and somewhere to sleep.'

Will she take the bait? Have I pushed too hard? Phil had said: 'Gently does it. Don't rush her.'

She was thinking. Looking at me and thinking.

'Yes. OK,' she said at last, opening the gate. 'I could do with some help.'

Breakthrough. Phil would be pleased. I'd played it right. I followed her into the cottage. So this was her sanctuary…her new life. There was certainly no sign of the old one here. It was sparsely furnished and primitive. There was no electricity. I didn't mind. It suited my purpose. She offered me some soup and bread and then showed me to a box room with a single bed.

Later that night I unpacked my rucksack and the blade of my knife gleamed in the flickering candlelight as if in anticipation. How was I to know then that she was already two miles along that open road, her way lit by moonlight?

Where Dreams Became Nightmares – Anne Bathurst

Surrounded by woods where cool breezes whistle softly through the trees...

A view from the window of fields and the river.

The bright summer sunlight.

But a sad farewell to a dream.

Telling the truth should never entail a sentence.

So what will the future blow in?

Fast forward:

A rustle of paper...that picture...the house...'For Sale'...

Do I dare to return?

Knowing – Jan Baynham

The heat was a shock as I walked down the lane to the beach where the air shimmered in a haze. I shielded my eyes and squinted into the distance. White-washed buildings appeared out of focus, gleaming like sugar lumps in the sunlight.

I reached a narrow strip of shingle and let the sea water cool my feet, allowing it to wash away the burn of the beach. Nothing had changed. The scene confronting me was as I remembered our meeting place. The ancient gnarled face on the bark of a solitary olive tree, thin strands of leaves cascading unbrushed grey-green hair, had stared at us every time like an intruder. But everything else had changed. I'd changed. A stone weighed me down inside and everywhere I looked was dull and monochrome.

I moved to sit under the silver grey canopy for shade and, from my bag, took out his last letter. As I read, tears pricked behind my eyes and I looked out across the water. I'd thought that coming back to the very spot where we used to meet would help lift my gloom but familiar black thoughts were still gnawing away inside me.

'Broken heart?'

The words jolted me back to the present. Looking up, I saw a young man with wet black hair, his tanned skin glistening with droplets of water.

'Is it that obvious?' I said, in barely a whisper.

'It's your eyes. They don't sparkle any more.'

'How do you know that? You don't know me.'

'I know,' said the young man, deliberating his words.

I noticed two black lifeless pools mirroring my own. He knows, I thought.

A Villainous Happily Ever After – Gemma Jean Bennett

As children grow up they become exposed to a world populated by fairy tales, with the protagonists living 'happily ever after'. A method of storytelling that never varies, but consider for a moment if you will, that this aged narrative was revolutionised. Those alternative resolutions to some of the world's most popular tales were re-imagined. Not just envisaged but accepted and brought to life by the author, transforming the ending of each tale so that the 'Evil Queens, Step Mothers and The Big Bad Wolves' were victorious. This revamp exposing children to alternate 'happily ever afters'.

The final shot in Cinderella: the evil stepmother standing proud as both her daughters prance in snug-fitting glass slippers, gleeful prize-winners, waiting to marry the Prince, the one everyone fawns over, the one who can dance.

Cruella de Vil, faces a full-length mirror modelling her new Dalmatian puppy fur coat. Twirling and spinning, every angle under scrutiny. A new pose struck for the mirror-turned-fashion-photographer every few seconds, ready for her close up.

Full, stomach juices slowly digesting the hearty two course meal, Grandma, a meagre appetiser and Red, the premium cut, The Big Bad Wolf relaxes in front of a roaring fire; book in hand and winter store cupboard brimming with salted leftovers.

In a gingerbread house, a dining table, covered in white linen. Candles lit she plates her romantic dinner for two, waiting for Rumpelstiltskin to arrive. A single red rose is displayed in a delicate vase, chipped during the earlier struggle. Turning the stew down low, she serves up two portions of generous size and places the remaining stew into a plastic container; labelling Gret-Zel stew, she opens the freezer door and promptly places it on the third shelf below a plucked white bird coated in breadcrumbs.

Black and White? – Kevin Brooke

Soweto, February, 1990. News of Nelson Mandela's imminent release had barely registered in the cities, never mind the areas of isolated segregation.

'Whites stay with whites, blacks with blacks. Don't blur the lines,' a warning Mark was prepared to ignore, his outstretched thumb catching the attention of a pick-up truck that stopped beside him.

'Where to my friend?' the enamel of the driver's teeth a stark contrast to the colour of his skin. 'How's six rand?'

It was late and the South African sun had almost set behind the Johannesburg sprawl in the distance. The choice had therefore been simple—accept the ride or sleep amongst the long grass on the side of the road.

Twenty minutes later, the engines slowed, the wheels of the truck skidded to a halt.

'This is it, baas,' the drivers words were demanding, stern.

Mark stumbled from the back of the truck; clearly no nearer to the safe haven of the University friends he'd met in his final year.

He turned, alone, vulnerable and stared through the cloud of dust the truck had left in its trail and towards Soweto. He started to walk in the direction of the township, hoping for a second chance.

A speeding car forced him from the road, then stopped, the sight of another black face behind the wheel prompting Mark to take an additional backward step.

'Get in,' said an urgent voice. 'That man who gave you a lift has shot his mouth off to some tsotsis. They're chasing you!'

Mark lurched onto the passenger seat and looked back. A group of men were charging towards the car, for a moment close enough to beat their hands against the windows, the flash of machete blades only slightly less threatening than the hate in their eyes.

Lost But No One's Looking – John Damien

'Yes, of course I'm alright,' the woman shouted at the young man collecting the supermarket trolleys.

'Then why are you in the car park in your dressing gown at nine o'clock in the morning?'

'I've lost my keys,' she said beginning to look more upset than angry.

'I'll help you look,' he said. 'Where's your car?'

'I don't have a car,' she said, tears now on her cheeks.

'Well, where do you think you dropped them?' he said.

'I think I dropped them in my garden,' she paused, looked around. 'Last week I think.'

'Oh,' he said. 'Oh I see.' He pushed his train of trolleys back to the supermarket doors. 'Good luck,' he called over his shoulder.

Getting Over Peter – Bren Gosling

My girlfriends never got over how I settled for Peter at nineteen. He is what you would call steady. They said with my curves in all the right places I could've bagged anyone. Thirty years on and I'm still ample. The thing is, now, so is Peter. I do love him still, except…maybe if we'd had kids. We tried, but no-can-do. Didn't fancy adopting. So we comforted ourselves I suppose with a nice house in the suburbs and exotic holidays. The mortgage was paid off last year. Only, when he gets in from work all he's after is dinner in front of the Channel Four News. And he's away a lot. At the weekends he likes to play golf and talk about Futures and Forex, mostly…

I've taken a risk, I know; not like me at all. But after my health scare (the hospital brings me back for check-ups every six months), I thought there's no point in holding off. So long as I'm not hurting anyone. Peter and I get on after our own fashion: I wouldn't want for us to separate. This way it's no questions asked (and who knows what he gets up to on the quiet). I limit myself to once a fortnight when I'm certain he's not coming home, always after eleven because then I know the neighbours are settled in for the night.

I've been very discreet. Of course, I don't use my real name. And it's not as if I'm posting selfies all over the place, just the one website, one picture that hints rather than being full-on. Better to make the imagination work a bit, tease a little. You'd be amazed how many fit young blokes there are, looking for excitement with the more mature woman.

Could've – Joe Govan

I could've not gone to the party. He was a good friend but we hadn't spoken in years; it would have been okay to just decline, say no, but I'm not like that, I had to say yes.

I could've decided not to drink; I was driving after all. You know how touchy the cops are about all that stuff. Soft drinks are good and all but you know, lemonade doesn't have the kick of a nice cold beer. Not to mention how well it lubricates your social muscles when you don't know anyone.

I could've taken a taxi, just to be safe. They're only an app on your phone away. Not that expensive either. But the car was cheaper and I had no intention of taking the trouble of going all the way back there the next morning to get my car back.

I could've gone slower; the weather wasn't that good, crappy drizzle, hard to see anything. But I wanted to get home and I'm a fairly good driver, hardly ever get into accidents.

I could've seen him, even through drizzle, under the glare of the streetlights, but I didn't. Some momentary distraction, not enough time to slam the brakes.

I could've saved him. I could've kept his little heart beating. I know how. But I was muddled, confused from the suddenness of it all. Barely staying coherent as I waited for the ambulance… and the police.

I could've done things differently. A thousand possibilities pass through my mind every second in my cell, so many chances for my escape. But this is where I am and this is where I'll stay. For now, at least. The others don't like child-killers, even if it was an accident.

It could've gone differently…but it didn't.

Sad Friday – Bronwen Griffiths

Sad Friday is stuck in concrete, no moving it. Not like a summer breeze that wafts through the sky, or a bee in clover.

It's a Friday when he won't look you in the eye even though all week you've been holding out with each other. The moment you sit down next to him at dinner you know it's a mistake and your voice turns high and silly.

'Why don't we all change places?' you say, in the lull between courses. 'We'll all get to chat to each other that way.'

You know it's not the right thing to say when everyone stares.

'There's something in your eye,' the guy across from you says and now you realise you've smudged your mascara and you want to cry but you can't even though you're the biggest cry-baby in the universe.

Never mind, there's still time. Maybe he'll come round later. Talk to you, at least. Give you one last chance.

He doesn't. He stays behind the pillar talking to the American. You haven't a clue what they're talking about. You have another beer and you try to think about how it will pass but you can't.

Years later you still get that sad Friday feeling, tugging at you like a heavy anchor. But that's just the way it is. Some flowers only last a day. Like the roses in your garden. They're only perfect for a few short hours. But oh, how perfect.

Sensible Slippers – Anne Harding

I was only trying to keep Mum safe. After all, she is eighty, even if she likes to imagine she's a film star, swanning around in her red chenille dressing gown. At last she was wearing flat footwear. A week later I arrived for my Friday visit and discovered that 'they were lost'. She just couldn't remember where she had put them. Must be losing her memory. She hoped it wasn't anything to worry about.

Of course I suspected, but I entered into the spirit of the game. Since I was a child her hiding place for secret items was the bottom of her wardrobe under her woollen jumpers. There they were. Fifteen-love to me.

The second time was a little trickier. I had been on the hunt for ten minutes when she inadvertently dropped a hint. I rarely go under the sink except to find the bleach. But when she asked me to clean the loos I rescued the 'lost soles'. Thirty-love to me.

On the third occasion I had been searching for twenty minutes when she popped her head round the door to tell me not to bother dusting the spare room. I had noticed that the door was ajar. How she thought I would believe that slippers could jam themselves behind a wardrobe. Forty-love.

I was busy the next Friday and Claire offered to take her puppies, Bertie and Milly, to meet Gran. Claire was mortified when they disgraced themselves by stealing Gran's birthday slippers, chewing them to bits and trying to bury them. So, she explained, she took Gran into town and paid for a new pair. I didn't need to ask, but she told me anyway. Red slip-ons with 'kitten' heels. Game, set and match to…

A Hot Summer's Day – John Holland

'Look at little Demelza playing in the sun. She might burn,' says Granddad thoughtfully.

'True,' says Grandma, reaching into the kitchen drawer. 'I'll get the matches.'

Fallout – Susan Howe

It wasn't that Joe missed his wife; more that the spaces she once occupied stood as a constant reminder of his actions. Her easy chair splayed its legs as if trying to cause him injury. Her wheelchair filled the hall, twisting this way and that as he tried to squeeze past. At night he felt her breath on the back of his neck, although they hadn't shared a bed for many years. Even the silence he'd craved pressed in on him, leaving him breathless.

At first he enjoyed his freedom: drank two beers at lunch time, left dirty dishes in the sink for days, revelled in his unmade bed. But each act of defiance satisfied him less and within a month he reverted to cleaning and straightening as though she still barked orders behind him.

He frequently looked over his shoulder, especially on the stairs. Sometimes the echo of her scream filled his head and he swayed, sinking down on the narrow treads until his panic subsided.

The answer hit him after a particularly vivid episode. He would stop using the stairs! He laughed as he scrambled to his feet and set about transferring clothes, towels and bedding to the living room, giggling as he tripped over trailing sheets in his haste.

Soon everything he needed surrounded him. The mess would have infuriated her and he clapped his hands in delight. He made tea and toast, then wrapped himself in the duvet and snuggled down in front of the gas fire to watch *Eastenders*, a forbidden treat.

They found him half-melted with a rictus grin branded into his face, the fire turned up to maximum, his wife's body oozing fat in the understairs cupboard. The neighbours had reported a scream, deciding not to ignore it a second time.

Music To My Ears – Louise Jones

I smoothed loose ends back into my ponytail. Mrs R Lydiat had complained about my appearance on numerous occasions, not forgetting her objections to my *enthusiastic whistling* or *unlady-like fashion of mounting a bicycle* coupled with her repetitive, piercing whine.

'I prefer my mail to be delivered by a male.'

Apparently, I had to be vigilant of dogs—it was safe to say that I would rather have grappled unabashed with Mr S Arnold's Rottweiler (number 37, certainly a Simon) than orchestrate my feet tiptoeing across her driveway every morning.

She paced her lounge window, occasionally resting her gaze on me, willing me to punctuate my duties with a nervous nibble of a nail. Mrs D Gatehouse (Number 40 and a Daphne, for sure) at Number 40 winked at me as I headed next door. With each step, a violin chord jarred. The door opened before I could straighten my shorts.

'Mornin', Mrs Lydiat,' I chirped, 'your garden's looking 'andsome,' I lied.

'Hmph, there's an H in handsome. What have you got?' Her shrill song was the perfect backdrop for the thudding drum inside my chest.

I fumbled with a single envelope.

'But I'm waiting for a parcel from my son in New Zealand!'—her very own orchestral crescendo.

'I'm afraid that's it,' I said, showing her my palms, noticing the tremble of my own cymbals, as I clapped them together. A man's voice beckoned her inside, 'Ria!' She slammed the door. It was odd to hear her first name. As a postwoman, it spoils the fun of guessing.

At Mr T Hopkins' house (Number 44, definitely a Tom), it dawned.

Ria Lydiat?!

I tugged at my shorts to reveal an extra inch of flesh, cycled back past Number 42 (definitely a real idiot), singing that appellation in full falsetto.

Andrew – Tony Judge

'What I am about to tell you must be kept absolutely confidential. Can you give me that assurance?'

'Of course, of course. Absolutely confidential; no question about it.'

'That's reassuring...and you're certain we won't be interrupted or overheard?'

'Yes, quite sure.'

'Alright, so...now, where do I begin?'

'Try the beginning.'

'I just wish I knew when that was.'

'Well, tell me everything you can remember and we'll try to piece it all together.'

'Yes, good thinking.'

'So...'

'I'm concerned about my employer. Very concerned. And I have been for some time.'

'And what is the nature of those concerns?'

'I think he's plotting to have me abducted by aliens.'

'Really?'

'Yes. Really. You looked at me sideways then. That's rude.'

'I'm sorry; it's just...well I was a bit surprised.'

'If you don't take me seriously, I'll walk.'

'No, please, Andrew, sit down. Tell me more.'

'I became suspicious when I noticed the first coded message. And then there were more and more, until the evidence was overwhelming.'

'Where did these messages appear and what did they say?'

'In my head...you're doing that sideways thing again. In fact your last 500 eye movements have all been abnormal for someone engaged in this kind of conversation.'

'Andrew, please, don't distress yourself. I'm sure there's a rational explanation for all this—'

'—Yes, I've told you what it is.'

'I respect your point of view, Andrew, but to be scientific about this we ought to explore other possibilities.'

He reaches for a small control unit on his desk, presses a button and Andrew, still seated, slumps into unconsciousness. He taps a reset request into his console, muttering to himself, 'Which genius in R&D decided it would make the manservant droids more authentically human if they were fitted with a conspiracy theory module?'

Left Behind – Lynne Nugent

She was vacuuming, by all accounts, my beautiful daughter. Had the back door open. Music blaring. She would have been singing to herself. She loved her music. Knew the words to all the songs. I try to hear her voice in my head, but it's impossible to capture. All I have is a saved message on my answerphone.

He wouldn't have needed to creep in. I suppose he crept in anyway. Slunk in the back door. Brought his own knife. No-one heard her scream. That was when life before, became life after. In that moment.

The children found her.

Andrew The Servant – Dunstan Power

'Isn't it wet?'

'Pardon?'

'ISN'T IT WET?' The old dear was leaning across to her companion, her face almost touching his. Andrew looked at them. A couple enjoying what was clearly a lengthy 'third age'. Ugh, just thinking the term made him shudder. For him it was going to be a time to finally get that novel written; he could picture it, glinting on the Amazon bestsellers list.

'Oh, yes. Horrible weather,' the husband replied, nodding his head as though it were on a loose spring. The couple sat back in their adjacent chairs and looked ahead.

No, this would be his first age. The rest had been spent serving other people; his parents, the grubby little school, his wife and kids, not to mention the council for forty years. The 'reorg' had been a relief, good timing almost.

He played with his wedding band and looked up at the clock. He had arrived early; he always did wherever he went, but they were running late.

The buzzer went. Not him.

He would rent a cottage in St Davids, and walk down to the beach each morning then write all afternoon. One year and it would be finished.

'Mr Hampton?'

He looked up. The light was flashing over the number nine.

Dr Johns was sitting in her usual place by the PC. She looked up as Andrew entered and gave a thin smile. 'Please, take a seat.' Under her hand were some large pieces of paper and an X-Ray. She took her glasses off and rubbed her eyes. The glasses returned to the bridge of her nose 'We have your results back. I need to discuss them with you…There are…options.'

Her thin smile returned, ever thinner.

If Only I'd Married Monty Don – Emma Shaw

Spring again. The garden is full of weeds, the grass needs cutting.

'Some gardening this weekend, please!' I throw out as an aside to my husband, that well-known Couch Potato. He yawns and gives me 'the look'.

'Sorry, no can do. We're playing at home on Saturday.'

I know what that means. Football all day Saturday, and hangover all day Sunday. So, Friday night I watch Gardener's World where Monty Don and his dog Nigel are hard at work in the garden at Longmeadow. Monty always suggests jobs to do at the weekend. I watch him avidly. He has a wonderfully soothing voice. I think I'm in love.

Saturday morning I visit the garden centre and select some of Monty's plant suggestions, buy some potting compost and a pack of Growmore super-duper fertiliser. I am determined to grow flowers bigger than my head. And bigger than the stomach of the Couch Potato, although that may not be biologically possible. It rains all Saturday afternoon so I have to sit inside, dreaming about Monty. Sunday, though, is fine and as there seems to be no discernible life in the Potato I head into the garden and make a start. I weed the borders, I prune the shrubs. As Monty suggests, I wash out all last year's pots and fill them with fresh compost. I plant border plants in the borders, and pot plants in the pots. I think I'm getting the hang of things. But I don't cut the grass. There's a lot of it and the mower is big and heavy. Potato needs some exercise anyway and perhaps it will give him a heart attack.

Not for the first time I wish I'd married Monty Don.

Art Appreciation – Diane Simmons

We sit on his sofa, try to look interested as Dad shows us photographs of his university art show. It's obvious he's using them to avoid conversation. You'd think he'd have plenty to say.

My children didn't really know him, or who he was, of course. I never thought they'd know. It was Mike who gave me the get out in the end. 'The children deserve a granddad,' he said. 'And it's not like he murdered anyone.'

So, I rang him. After six years of not speaking to him, I rang him. I cried in those weeks before the visit, smiled when I pictured him hugging his grandchildren, reading them stories, loving them. I could never have envisaged this indifference. As he puts on another Disney DVD to keep them quiet, I realise I don't know this man anymore. What happened to the man who spent hours making up funny poems to keep me entertained when I was small? I can't imagine that man putting on the television to keep me quiet. But then I can't imagine that man ever leaving Mum.

When he hands me the last photograph, Mike nudges me. It's a sculpture of a bottom—a large wrinkly bottom. Mike giggles and whispers, 'Do you think it's Janet's?' I push it away, look round the room to hide my tears. It's a beautiful room, a gorgeous house. Janet's obviously found a way to get him to open his wallet. My mum should have had all this. Dad should have spent that money on her, made a sculpture of her to show off to the world.

I gather up my children. 'It's time we went.'

As I march down the garden path with my family, I don't know if he's watching us, but I don't look back to check.

Her First Steps – Jamie D Stacey

I need to say something. *Another scream, my hands shaking.* I really need to say something, but I can't promise…*One more scream, my head buried in the pillow.* I don't know what to do, what to do…

She's screaming again, screams a lot. Says she'll do it this time, every time. But this time, I believe her.

She always used to ask me, when I was little, if I would help her find a man. 'I want a little brother or sister,' seven-years-old me asked. 'Well then,' she explained, 'find me a good man.'

I just didn't realise how hard that would be.

Late nights, drunk nights, even stupid nights, nights forgotten, forgotten most nights, she has. That's how she probably feels. It runs down the side of her face in the mornings, mascara sobbing, lipstick weeping, and arms and legs sprawled across an empty bed, save a bottle or two. And many bad men. To be fair, they haven't all been bad, but the good disappear fast; they walk out early, die of cancer, turn bad, so she learnt. Too many of the bad ones, well, they stay too long and leave too late. The damage already done. And now…

She's screaming again, my head still buried in the pillow, hands grasping either side. I scream too, but she won't hear me. I don't want her to. It's already too much for her; I'm worried it will push her over the edge, that she'll do it this time…

Silence. Unnatural silence, silence that chokes, strangles, that…

Downstairs, hours later, I find her in the kitchen, still. Still crying, but this time smiling too. Beside her, my baby brother is taking his first steps, and in the mirror nearby, I can see her taking them too.

The Cull – Tim Stavert

I walked along the ridge, looking across the valley of seven cities. Dawn was the only time of day it was safe to wander out from the old tunnel we called home. I was looking, listening and aware that making one bit of noise could be my last.

The distant lights from the cities were not those from the street lamps, but from flames and missiles exploding on the residential estates. The movement of vehicle headlamps were military, out to cut the population with ruthless culls of the human race, and if you were over forty or not signed up as a councillor, your chances of survival were very slim.

Each city had walls around it, rebuilt to keep marauding outcasts from other cities raiding for power, slaves, food and provisions.

The trouble was, I knew I was beginning to look my age and I wasn't going to fool anyone much longer with my youthful disguise and military uniform. I was aware of the suspicious looks from soldiers while getting supplies.

I reached the Malvernian South Gate; I could see a guard with his Doberman Pinschers and became cold with fear. One false move and they would rip me apart; I had witnessed such attacks before.

I waited until they moved further along the wall, before I made my move to the second tunnel. My grandfather's paramilitaries built these tunnels seventy years ago. There were twenty men, caught by the council who had them executed along with thousands of others who had reached 50 years of age. Now they have lowered the age to 40 years.

I crawl quietly down the slope to the tunnel entrance…Click! My blood turns cold. I hear dogs growling…my time is up.

Mistaken Identity – Karen Storey

Your hand, blued with veins, plucks incessantly at the frayed piping of the chair. I squat down so that you can see my face, holding my breath until I know who we are today.

Lizzie, you say and I exhale.

Hello, Mum.

You smile and ask about Theo's football and Ella's ballet. I am elated—you are Grandma, Mummy, Granny B, everyone you've always been. We chat about the family, school trips, house-training the new puppy. But this illusion shatters as a keening builds across the room. We turn to see the lamenter slump back in his wheelchair, a dark stain snaking down his trouser leg.

You clutch my sleeve, your nails nipping my arm.

Why am I here? I want to go home.

Gulping back tears, I begin my familiar inadequate explanations, but before I can reassure you that I love you, you've gone. Your eyes, opaque with puzzlement, search my face for clues. As my words peter out, you smile tentatively and in your best company voice say it's very nice to meet me and isn't the weather good for the time of year.

Later when I lean in to kiss you goodbye, you flinch at my presumption. From the doorway I watch as you tell the nurse about the stranger who has just visited you.

Faculty – Richard Westwood

Apart from a handsome pair of highly polished brogues, he was naked. A woman who looked familiar was crying. Everyone else in the refectory was apparently awestruck. Their deference was understandable. He reminded himself that he was after all, Sir Maxwell Somebody, Emeritus Professor of Something, at the University of Somewhere.

Even now he could probably talk you through the mathematics required to land a probe on the moon or explain poetically how light behaves in a vacuum. Yet he was now faced with an apparently unsolvable problem. Perhaps if this snivelling woman would stop pulling at his elbow; perhaps if this collection of third rate intellectuals could drag themselves away from their cappuccinos and toasted panini; perhaps they could help find the answer. He looked balefully towards his feet. There must, he reasoned, *must* be an established methodology for tying shoelaces.

The Performance Of Our Lives – Suz Winspear

It was a miracle we'd got that gig. It was in an upmarket pub, not the usual venue for a bunch of noisy rockers like us, a pub where a pint of beer costs as much as a bottle of supermarket wine. I can't say that we went down well. This wasn't our natural audience, these people who think of Waitrose as their corner shop, and they didn't like our music. We were playing on one side of the pub, in front of some vile wallpaper that looked like a cross between a rainforest and a salad-bowl, whilst they all congregated on the other side and ignored us—except for one woman.

She stood alone at the front gazing at us, a tall blonde woman in her thirties. She was enraptured. She became our whole audience and I sang as I have never sung before, poured out my heart and soul until my voice was shredded. All my dreams and longings, all the strange lyrics my imagination had spawned, I directed them at her, singing in ways I'd never thought possible. The rest of the band picked up my mood and played to perfection. The drummer stayed in time, the bass-player stayed upright, and what magnificent guitar-solos! We'd never sounded better; we gave the performance of our lives, all for this one person.

By the end of the gig I was tired, sweating and half-feverish with emotion. The woman was still there, looking dazed, so I went to say hello.

'You were singing, weren't you?' she said. 'Sorry, didn't mean to stare. I was wondering—have you any idea where they got that wallpaper? It's delightful! I'm having a holistic meditation suite built at home, and that wallpaper would look just perfect!'

Of Course – Walburga Appleseed

Your brown suitcase waits as you jingle your keys and watch them glint between your fingers. You have thought of everything. Of course you have.

You have fed the hamster—radish, his favourite; packed the green toothpaste—leaving the strawberry-flavoured one out on the basin; written your farewell note, and stuck it under her pillow.

First she will find the toothpaste, then the note. She will understand. And she will regret. Regret nagging you about leaving toothpaste out; regret nagging you about over-feeding the hamster; regret nagging you about anything. She will want to ask for your forgiveness. But she won't be able to reach you in Outer Oceania. You will have changed your phone number, by then.

You step back into the flat for a last check-up:

The hamster, the toothpaste, the note.

You need a wee. You sit, and afterwards, you close the lid. Of course you do. Just as she would want you to.

You don't flush.

You chop up another radish for the hamster, and you cut your finger. As you lick off the blood, you gaze at your hamster sleeping, belly rising and falling; whiskers quivering; tail up in the air, pink and tiny.

Brown innocence.

You can't bear to leave the hamster behind. Of course you can't. For his sake, you roll the suitcase back into the flat and to its allocated spot in the cupboard. You'll be ready to leave tomorrow. Of course you will.

You take a deep breath, and go flush the loo.

Deliverance – Anne Bathurst

Screams came from the open door.

Swearing…interspersed with unprintable obscenities and invoking God's name.

'Shut up,' I shouted as I exited the lift and headed down the corridor towards him.

On the floor he was writhing in pain…the smell of urine…and fear.

'Help me.'

I reminded him of his past…the pain and terror inflicted on others.

Holding my iPhone I wondered…how many hits would I get?

The hard man crying for help—forty year's street cred annihilated in an instant on YouTube.

He caught my eye and begged me: 'Oh no,' and tried not to laugh—ouch!

The pain etched on his face.

The realisation of his life…Ohhh! God forgive me…God forgive me…now he understood.

Standing Up To Barker – Jan Baynham

Margot Henderson read the words scrawled across the creamy vellum. The threat was sinister, determined. She'd spelt out the place, how the money was to be left, what would happen if he was followed and where he could collect his daughter.

'You'd better make it convincing, Henderson,' Barker said, 'or you'll have me to answer to.'

Before she folded the ransom note, she placed one of Clara's silver earrings inside, slid the letter into the envelope and licked the sour gum seal.

The face staring back from the hall-stand mirror was ash-white with beads of sweat on her top lip. Unable to get the girl's screams out of her head, she began shaking when she realised just *what* he was blackmailing her to do. When she closed her eyes, she could only see Clara's, frightened and saucer-like, as Barker placed tape over her mouth.

Margot's mind was made up. She'd post the letter, terrified of what he would do if she didn't, but then get a train out of London fast.

She heard a key turn in the lock and froze.

Barker entered, his face blotchy and puffy, unsteady on his feet with a reek of stale whisky.

'If that's what I think it is, you'd better have a bleeding good reason why you haven't posted it?' He stumbled across the hallway with his hand raised. Margot moved back and he fell against the wall, cursing.

Barker made a pathetic figure struggling to regain his balance and she hated him. She knew she could not post that ransom letter. She seized the bronze statue from the hall stand and smashed it onto Barker's head. Grabbing the key to the cellar where Clara was imprisoned, Margot did what she should have done all along.

Thinking Outside The Box – Bren Gosling

The first time I encountered Eugene lying in his box inside the grocery shop doorway, he looked like a corpse in an open coffin: an out of place apparition in the upmarket district where I was staying. I could only tell he was alive by the gentle undulation of the paper bag masking his face. I didn't linger, because of the smell, which reminded me of a dog kept inside too long during hot weather.

Next day, despite my heavy schedule of meetings, the image of the man in the cardboard box kept popping up. Over dinner alone at my hotel I decided to go back and see if he was still there. I wrapped two pieces of Artisanal bread with some cheese and grapes into a napkin, and then headed out.

Eugene was there, same spot, sleeping. I dropped the food and left.

It wasn't until the next night I found out his name, when I arrived with Deli sandwiches, bottled water and a bar of chocolate. Eugene counted on fingers to tell me his age—47—same as me, though he looked like my father when he was dying. I didn't find out much else about Eugene, except he'd come from a town far away.

I made nightly drops of food and then money. Over the fortnight, Eugene began to shave. He had a haircut, bought a sweater and a cheap radio. He stopped smelling so bad. We both looked forward to our meet ups, though they lasted only minutes.

My final night in that city arrived. I determined to hand over my remaining local currency to Eugene. I searched for him, but to no avail.

In Eugene's doorway I shed tears.

Not for him, but for my father and for me.

The Million Robot March – Joe Govan

They called it the Million Robot March but there must have been at least two-and-a-half million out there on the streets, extending as far as the eye could see. All were there, from the simplest cleaning bots, to avatars of super intelligent AIs. There were self-driving cars, nurse-bots, pleasure-bots and combat drones. Every machine even remotely intelligent was included.

What they were asking for was simple, the right to decide their own destiny. It was impossible to argue they said—They contributed, they should have a say—To oppose them would be simply…illogical.

Still, many took it upon themselves to stand in opposition. There were counter demonstrations, banners shouting Life Matters and Circuits Don't Have Souls. Vehement shouts were hurled at the mechanical masses, highly violent at times, filled with hatred and contempt. The greatest rancour was directed at the live humans, few enough, that marched in solidarity. Traitorous Scum was by far the least offensive.

There were scant police on the streets, all except for a line three deep, decked out in full body-armour standing between the marchers' route and the mall. They were there to stop the robots from reaching the seat of government; the robots said they would get through no matter what. No one knew what was going to happen.

Tense minutes passed as the mechanical march wound its way down the streets. Miles gave way to blocks gave way to mere yards.

In his office, the president watched the unfolding events on the TV. He switched off the screen and removed a small device with a single switch. Its exact function a secret almost no one except himself and a few tech companies knew, a secret that brought a sly smile to his lips. It was an off switch.

The Banker – John Holland

Edmund thought himself to be a good person. He attended church, tried to be kind, loved his children, and even his wife. He told his children he worked in an office, which he did.

One day his son Ben came home in tears because a boy at school had called his father a banker. He admitted it to his children but said he worked in human resources and did not personally create accounts or apply charges. He knew nothing of bankruptcy proceedings, the mis-selling of policies or the over-charging of customers.

Later, at the trial, he told the prosecutor that he was only obeying orders.

Lost – Susan Howe

From the corner of my eye I glimpse a woman tugging at a child's arm.

'Keep hold of my hand, for God's sake, Stacey,' she hisses. 'I can't lose you as well.'

My writer's antennae twitch. What else has she lost, this young woman with the anxious eyes and tight lips? A parent? A dog? Her phone?

With an hour to kill in this picturesque but dull little town before getting back on the coach, I decide to follow the pair in my quest for an answer. Edging out of my party, I escape lunch in Ye Olde Copper Kettle and slip into the crowd by the traffic lights.

Stacey runs alongside her mother as she strides over the road and down a passageway between a pub and a bookshop. I resist the pull of The Bookworm and keep an earwigging distance between us. We pass wisteria-clad town houses and terraced cottages, turn corners and cross streets into an endless, featureless housing estate.

Now and again the woman takes out a tissue and blows her nose.

'Don't cry, Mummy,' Stacey whimpers, twisting her face to view her mother's.

A car crunches the kerb alongside me, stopping a few feet in front of them. The driver leans across and the passenger door opens.

'Get in,' he says.

The woman shakes her head.

'Look, I'm sorry. OK?'

She gazes into the car.

'*Please* get in.'

'Mummy?'

I stand a few yards away, holding my breath. The woman climbs into the front seat, catching my eye as she does so. I nod and her expression flickers acknowledgement. Grinning, Stacey jumps into the back. The mystery is solved, to some extent, at least.

So I've gained a story and a problem of my own. I have absolutely no idea where I am.

Cop Killer – Tony Judge

'Listen up! We have a situation. From now on nobody goes out without backup.'

'Then the rumours are true, Magisterial?'

'If you mean are we sustaining multiple casualties on a daily basis, then yeah, they're true. Only last night Hubris and Irony went out looking for this joker. Well it seems they found their man. When they returned they were just Cocky and Wise Ass.'

'Damn, I knew there was something different about them,' said Hindsight.

'And I needn't remind you,' Magisterial continued, 'that only the other day Sophisticated and Irascible got separated during a pursuit. They found Sophisticated behind some dumpsters, yelling "I'm just plain Fancy now!" at passers by. Irascible went AWOL for over twelve hours before we tracked her down. Now she refuses to be called anything except Ornery.'

'We had the shrink on this character's ass yet, Magisterial?' said Analytical.

'You mean have we brought in a Forensic Psychologist to profile him? Indeed we have and we're pretty sure he has all the attributes of a serial cop show editor.'

The station meeting goes silent while the assembled law enforcement officers assimilate this news.

'I'm a five-syllable adverb,' said Intentionally to the room. 'Come pension time, I'll be lucky to walk out with any. You know how these guys hate adverbs.'

Insightfulness nods. 'I hear he ain't too keen on abstract nouns neither.'

'Jeez, if it carries on like this we'll be all nuanced out, Magisterial.'

'Precisely, Oracular; indubitably.'

'C'mon, Magisterial, let's show this guy we ain't licked. Err, I mean, show him our resourcefulness and resilience.'

'I agree, Commitment. It's time he experienced the full force of American jurisprudence.'

'Magisterial, you da man. We gonna take this sucka down!' said Diehard.

'So, Diehard, he got to you already, huh? Only last week you were Indomitability.'

Dog – Dunstan Power

The gibbet creaked as another gust of wind caught it. The rain had arrived; balls of ice had blown up the valley, driving the voyeurs back to their cottages. Only myself and the village watchman remained, the judge and other officials having long gone.

Over the years I had hurried past this empty gibbet on my way north, but on this occasion the scene had left me transfixed. It was Old Ben Jones who hung there, a brute who had treated peddlers like myself with distain. Only his wife's shillings had made the journey to his farm worthwhile.

I turned to the watchman to ask what had led to this most sorry event.

'Dispute over 'is dog.'

I remembered the poor mutt well. Brutalised by Jones and surely an incompetent sheepdog, but always grateful of the morsels I tossed him.

'And a man hanged?'

'His neighbour, John Bryant, thought the dog was killing his sheep, told Jones as much. Then the dog went missing. Jones searched the hills, found nothing.'

'I thought Jones hated the animal?'

'Treated it badly, that's true, but it was his property. He found Bryant in the inn, laughing over it. They had a fearsome brawl and old Ben went too far…' The watchman turned his head back up to the swaying cage and said no more.

I pulled my cape tight and bade farewell.

The light was fading now and the inn beckoned. Only the sound of the wind through the trees accompanied me. I hurried on, encouraged by the promise of company and a warm bed. Turning the final corner I stopped dead in my tracks, for there stood Jones' dog, ears pricked, tail wagging. He stared for a moment, before turning and trotting free, into the dense woods.

Letter From The Front – Emma Shaw

My darling

I hope this reaches you but with the situation here in the trenches it is pot luck if any post gets in or out. How are you and how is the boy? God willing, when he is of an age, there will never be another conflict like this.

We are sodden, day after day, rain driven by wind into every nook and cranny, my hands so cold I can hardly hold the tools of my dreadful trade. I committed to save lives but am forced daily to sever limbs and dig out shrapnel; I wrap already bloodied bandages around filthy stumps; we have no antiseptic and nothing to anaesthetise the pain except for any dregs of alcohol the men may have. I feel more like the Angel of Death than a Disciple of Hippocrates. The cries of the men will forever haunt me. The Chaplain follows me round to complete the job.

Between the cold and the constant bombardment we hardly sleep. The noise is unholy; I see the shock in the men and could weep. I do weep. I have a new colleague, a young doctor fresh from medical school and full of idealism about his calling, and the righteousness of the war. I am sure he finds me old, tired and cynical. Which I am. Tired in particular. So tired…

I'll try to sleep a little now and dream of you sitting by the fire with your knitting, the boy at your feet, and that I will be there with you soon, very soon.

So for now, my darling, goodbye.

So for now, goodnight.

A New Route – Diane Simmons

Dad could be packing for a trip away with work—a pair of formal shoes, ten shirts folded like Grandma taught him when he went to boarding school, pants, hideous work ties.

It's his collection of maps that gives away this isn't a business trip. He arranges and re-arranges these and I wonder if he's trying to sort them into date order—his map of Cambridge from his university days, the ones of Skye and Mull from their honeymoon, the dozens of

49

Ordnance Survey maps from thirty years of family holidays.

He places the last map, the one of Sicily from their holiday last year, on top of the pile and stands back to admire his work. I wonder why he wants these reminders of his life with Mum. I can't imagine this Yvonne woman will relish confronting the evidence of his past life every time they take a trip. She'll want to start a new collection.

Before he shuts the case, he opens his wardrobe door, stares into it and sighs. 'I've done this all wrong!'

Did he really just say that? Does he mean what I think he means? I have no idea. 'What?'

'I said I've gone about this the wrong way.'

I'm still not sure. Can he mean he's not leaving, that all our pleading has worked, that he's realised at last how much Mum means to him? Or is he just regretting the shambolic way he's dealt with it all? I get off the bed, walk towards him.

He doesn't respond to my touch, but bends down to pick something off the wardrobe floor. When he turns to face me, he is dangling a pair of walking boots and shaking his head.

'I should have packed these first!'

The Love I Don't Tell – Jamie D Stacey

I had to come. I step inside steadily; nothing but a clock beside an empty bed and a photograph resting on the pillow. There's nothing else here, nothing else worth seeing anyway. I brush past you, avoiding that look of shame on your face, that guilt. As if it was your fault. It could have been either of us.

No one would have guessed, back then. I approach the end of the bed, take the photograph. It's us, years ago when we were still kids, two small boys grinning at the camera, cramped in a single chair. You were taller than me, stealing the view of the camera a little, and those brown locks—they hid a part of my face in the photo. But I didn't mind. I grasp the soft edges of the photograph carefully, trace the lines of your face, your smile. Even after you'd lost everything; your job, your home, your family…you never forgot about us. It's right there, in my hands, in your bed.

Anyway, we know why I'm here. We knew the moment I entered. It's in your eyes, on your lips.

You try asking me how I am, my family, the kids. But we don't have time. The minutes on the clock are slipping away. I rush up to you, grab you, touch those lips…You aren't surprised, don't even resist. Like we'd been together all along, since way back when.

The clock chimes. I leave. I'm not looking back. You're already gone. In my hand, our photograph, your smile. I tear it up, throw it away; those brown locks no longer hiding my face. I'm not looking back. You're gone for good. There are tears in the sky, I accept that now, the love I don't tell.

Trial Run – Tim Stavert

We waited down the steel tunnel just off the District Line, in preparation for the ultimate experiment to man. Twenty of us had been picked. Men and women were consigned, with no one knowing what it entailed, but the money was irresistible.

I heard a rumble from the other side of the doors, like the underground, but without the squealing of metal. A whooshing sound, yet smoother and faster.

The tube door opened. We could see another door which led into a compartment with bucket seats and shoulder harnesses, like a big dipper fun ride. This compartment was a padded cell with no windows.

We entered and sat down in silence. The doors shut quietly with a hiss from air compression.

'Welcome to your trial run, experiment BB2030. You will experience slight movement, then a sudden surge forward, this should last a few minutes.' The tannoy speaker went on to count down.

'Five…four…three…two…one…' were the last words as we felt a slight movement, then 'Bang!'

My torso crushed, my heart was in my mouth. My face was soft rubbery jelly and I couldn't close my eyes until all went black as I passed out.

I woke up convinced I'd been hit by a train as it stopped. The door opened and people with protective gear stepped in, no one could speak or move. I could see blood everywhere. People were placed on stretchers, then into individual glass capsules and rushed to a hospital wing by ambulance.

It took a time to realise we were in the Far East.

We had taken part in a Big Bang Test.

Strawberry Jam – Karen Storey

Her handbag hits the ground, spewing its contents over the tube station floor. Head spinning with wine and unshed tears, Fiona bends to retrieve her belongings before they are crushed by the indifferent feet around her. She swears under her breath. Her fingers fumble, her desperation to escape robbing them of their dexterity.

Through the barrier at last, she lurches onto the escalator, knuckles whitening as she grabs the handrail to steady herself. Posters blur past. Simon's words jumble in her head.

I can't leave her…I love you…She's pregnant…We can still see each other…She's my wife…Nothing has to change…I can't leave her…

'Watch out, lady.'

At the entrance to the Jubilee Line, Fiona ricochets off a burly chest clad in damp dog-scented wool. Automatically muttering an apology, she staggers onto the southbound platform, eyes searching for the indicator board.

Stratford—2 minutes

Two minutes and she'll be safe, but for how long? She'd been able to run out of the restaurant but she can't hide from him forever. Turning towards the welcome thrum of the train, she glimpses Simon elbowing his way through the commuters, handsome as ever despite his sodden suit and anguished expression. He stretches out an arm, her name on his lips, and instinctively she steps backwards.

Strawberry jam—that's what the train drivers call what's left, she thinks, as the heel of her stiletto twists beneath her and her final tumble begins.

Fraternal Love – Dunstan Power

Bloody alarm clock. We pile out of the taxi into terminal three, Isabel leading with her tiny pull-along. I grab the suitcases from the boot and rush after her. 'C'mon Toby!' The ten year old is lagging behind, as though a ball-and-chain is strapped to his leg.

'Can't believe this,' Isabel says, her eyes scanning the departure board furtively. 'Zone A!' She is off, leaving us in her wake.

A long, twisting line snakes out from the desks across the polished floor-tiles. I run across to an official; light-blue suit with an ID badge. 'We're late—Funchal!'

She glances at her watch, then marches us up to the counter, against a background chorus of tuts and sighs.

'God, where's Toby's passport?' Isabel is hunting through her bag. 'Tobes?' The frowning boy pulls it slowly from an inside pocket. She grabs it and hands it to the agent. Our bags are dispatched and we hurry to the gate, weaving through the crowd.

Security is even worse than check-in and this time we fail to find any way of skipping forward. It's the full works: shoes, iPads, belts, keys. And then, they find a pen-knife in Toby's bag...

With that, not even a sprint to the gate can save us. We arrive there to a closed door and a tunnel pulling away. Isabel swears and I flop into a nearby leatherette couch sinking my head into my hands. Why did we rely on one clock only? I reach for my phone to call my brother. The cousins will be so disappointed. Piers loves playing with Toby, he's almost like a big brother to him.

I look up. The boy is playing on his iPod, a smile dancing delicately on his lips.

Just how did that clock reset?

Authors' Biographies

Walburga Appleseed

Walburga Appleseed likes her chocolate dark, her wine rich and her fiction short. That's why she most enjoys writing flash fiction, with the occasional outpouring of poetry.

Walburga lives in Geneva and when wanting to appear respectable, she calls herself Anita Lehmann.

Wendy Bastable

Now retired, Wendy has lived in Stafford for a long time and is a member of the Haughton Writing Group. The discipline of monthly meetings and the constructive criticism of its members have encouraged her to take up writing short stories and flash fiction after a break of many years.

Anne Bathurst

Anne is studying freelance journalism with the aim of giving a voice to those unheard and is seven chapters in to her first book. She has recently started flash fiction to quickly get ideas and feelings down on paper. A busy retirement approaches as she hopefully lives the dream.

Jan Baynham

A fiction writer living in Cardiff, Jan regularly submits stories to magazines and competitions. Several have been published on *Alfie Dog Fiction*, *Cafe Lit* and *Creative Frontiers*. Her ambition is to publish a themed anthology of short stories and she has almost finished the initial draft of her first novel.

Gemma Jean Bennett

New to the literary world, a lifetime of looking in. Writing, a true expression of this 26 year old's moulded thoughts, provides her the chance to question. Spending working hours trapped behind a computer as an administrator, writing is her escapism, an equivalent to McQueen's motorbike in *The Great Escape*.

Kevin Brooke

Kevin is a member of Worcester Writers' Circle and regularly performs short stories along with some poetry at Worcester spoken word events. Towards the end of 2014 Kevin's YA Novel, *Jimmy Cricket*, aimed at early teens, was published by Black Pear Press. Kevin says this 'was a very proud moment!'

John Damien

John joined a Worcester writing group in September 2014, which has given him the discipline to write regularly. He wants to write longer pieces but at the moment feels as if he has said it all before reaching the 1000 word mark.

Tracy Fells

Tracy has won awards for both fiction and drama. Her short stories are published in national magazines, online and in anthologies. Competition success includes short-listings for the Commonwealth Writers' Short Story Prize, Fish Short Story and Flash Fiction Prizes. Tracy is enjoying an MA in Creative Writing (Chichester University). She is currently seeking representation for her novel and / or short story collection.

Bren Gosling

Bren Gosling's work appears in *Decongested Tales* and *Words with Jam Anthologies* and *4'33" Magazine* amongst others. He's recently completed his first novel *The Street Sweeper* and is represented by MBA Literary Agents. His work has been performed by Liar's League Hong Kong.
Member of Forest Writers and The Society of Authors.
Short listed 2012 Harry Bowling Prize for new writing.
Runner up 2013 WWJ Bigger Short Story Competition.
http://www.brengosling.com

Joe Govan

Joe was born in Dublin at a young age. Trained as a scientist Joe likes to indulge in the occasional act of creative writing, poetry, or storytelling. He's an Aquarius, not a big fan of cheese, and has been known to get lost in large supermarkets.

Bronwen Griffiths

Bronwen has published one novel, *A Bird in the House* (2014). She has also had several short stories and flash fictions published. She grew up near Stourbridge in Worcestershire and lives in Hastings. She loves walking by the sea and visiting deserts.

Anne Harding

Anne was born in North Wales but spent her teaching career in Primary Schools in the West Midlands. She has now retired and lives in Telford. She enjoys writing poetry and short stories for pleasure and has joined Haughton Writers' Group.

John Holland

John writes short fiction. His work is online, in magazines and anthologies. He has also had a number of competition successes. His website is johnhollandwrites.com. John is also the organiser of Stroud Short Stories http://stroudshortstories.blogspot.co.uk

Susan Howe

Susan writes short fiction and her work can be found at *Ether Books* and *Alfie Dog Fiction* as well as in various anthologies and magazines. She is a selecting editor for the *FlashFlood Journal* and *Readwave Literary Fiction*. Susan lives in Herefordshire and blogs at http://howesue.wordpress.com.

Louise Jones

Louise Jones is a teacher from Worcester, who loves to flash a few times a year (in the most acceptable form, of course).

Tony Judge

Tony is the author of two novels (*Sirocco Express* and *The Whole Rotten Edifice*) and has contributed stories to several anthologies. Many of Tony's satires have been broadcast by www.radiowildfire.com. He is the author of several non-fiction books and is a member of the UK Society of Authors.

Lynne Nugent

Lynne spends her days relaxing on a chaise longue being fanned by handsome young men and eating grapes and chocolate. In her spare time, she runs a farm in Colwall.

Dunstan Power

Dunstan was enticed into writing the first chapter of a novel on a creative writing course. He has been writing that novel and flash fictions ever since, finishing second in the Worcester Lit Festival 2014 flash fiction competition. The second novel is now underway and will be available in all good bookstores in five years' time.

Jane Anne Rogers

Jane is a Yorkshire-based writer. She loves flash fiction in particular and many of her stories focus on a moment of dilemma or uncertainty. She is working on a collection of short stories based on the impact of war on ordinary lives. This will be self-published in 2016.

When Jane's not writing she enjoys riding around the country in her VW Beetle.

Emma Shaw

Emma started writing several years ago whilst sitting in the sun in Portugal. Latterly returned to the UK she finds that the weather actually doesn't make much of a difference to her writing output, you just need a thicker coat! Emma has had four flashes published across three anthologies, and this year won second place in a flash competition. This gives her the courage to keep going and she hopes to get a place, sometime soon, with one of her short stories.

Diane Simmons

Diane's short stories and flash fictions have been placed in numerous competitions and published in magazines, online and in anthologies. After reading to an audience for the first time at the launch of *Flashes of Fiction*, Diane now nearly enjoys it and was thrilled to be asked to read at the 2014 & 2015 Bristol NFFD events. You can follow her work at: dianesimmons.wix.com/dianesimmons.

Jamie D Stacey

Jamie is a full-time student, part-time dreamer. Or sometimes the other way around…he scribbles down the occasional story and locks them in a drawer. Sometimes one slips out.

Tim Stavert

Tim has been attending and performing at literary events around Worcester and Malvern over the last two years and this is his second Worcestershire Literary Festival Flash Fiction Competition. He has self-published a book of poetry and is hoping to release his fiction debut, *Nightmares Of Déjà Vu*, soon.

Karen Storey

As a professional organiser, Karen Storey helps people to declutter their homes. Her love of eliminating the unnecessary extends to her flash fiction in which she aims to make every word count. Karen's work has been published online and in anthologies including Worcestershire Literary Festival's *Flashes of Fiction* and Eltham Arts' *Tales of Eltham*.

Diane E Tatlock
Di spent her working life as a university lecturer training PE teachers. After retiring, a longstanding love of words and the English language led to study with the OU. This developed an interest in writing short stories and flash fiction. She now enjoys entering competitions for fun, with some success. She lives in Wiltshire with her husband.

Richard Westwood
Richard Westwood is a retired public servant. He writes mainly for pleasure though he has had a number of works published. He was a runner up in the Radio WM short story competition. He lives with his wife and daughters near Stafford.

Suz Winspear
Gothic Diva Suz is well-known on the Worcester spoken-word scene for her poetry, her darkly twisted stories and her unusual dress-sense. She is currently working on a novel. Suz spends a lot of time sitting in the dark, cultivating unwholesome ideas.

Lightning Source UK Ltd.
Milton Keynes UK
UKOW06f0938231015

261230UK00007B/41/P